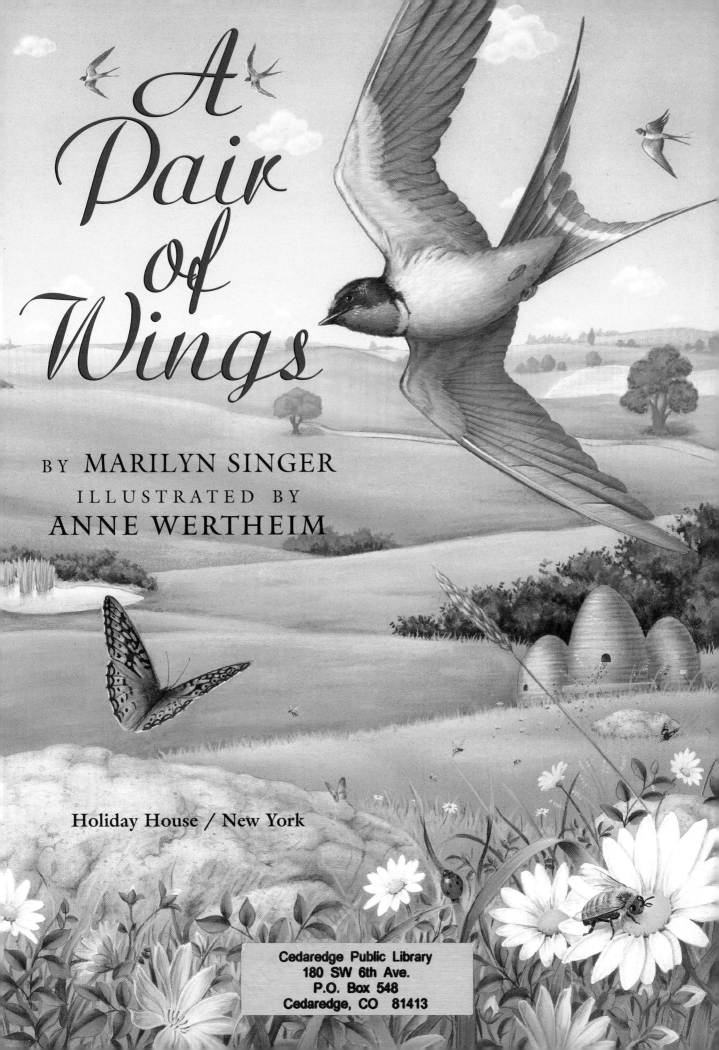

A Pair of Wings

BY MARILYN SINGER

ILLUSTRATED BY
ANNE WERTHEIM

Holiday House / New York

To fellow bird-watcher
and wonderful editor,
Mary Cash.
M. S.

To David
A. W.

eagle

Words in *italic* type in the text may be found in the glossary on page 29.

ACKNOWLEDGMENTS

Many thanks to Steve Aronson, Renee Cafiero, Barry Koffler, the staff at Holiday House, Dorothy Hinshaw Patent, and four wonderfully helpful scientists at the American Museum of Natural History: ornithologists Allison Andors and Jackie Weicker and entomologists Eric Quinter and Louis Sorkin.

blue jay

Library of Congress Cataloging-in-Publication Data
Singer, Marilyn.
A pair of wings / written by Marilyn Singer; illustrated by Anne Wertheim.—1st ed.
p. cm.
Includes bibliographical references (p.).
ISBN 0-8234-1547-3 (hardcover)
l. Wings—Juvenile literature. [1. Wings. 2. Animal flight.
3. Flight.] I. Wertheim, Anne, ill. II. Title.
QL950.8 .S56 2001
591.47'9—dc21   00-035078

ladybug

blue tit

peacock butterfly

arctic tern

great horned owl

If you had wings, what kind would they be?
Long and transparent as a dragonfly's?
Feathery and silent as an owl's?
Leathery and pointed as a bat's?
Would you use your wings to soar? To skim? To hover? To swim?
Or would you hardly use them at all?

hummingbird

small blue butterfly

dragonfly

western tanager

bumblebee

People have always wanted wings—to travel farther and faster, to ride the skies, to see the world from a brand-new view. We know that animals with wings can do many things other creatures can't.

They can find food in places other animals can't get to. They can nest in branches, on cliffs, or near the tops of skyscrapers. They can sleep in trees, on islands, or hanging from the ceilings of caves.

Animals that fly can often escape enemies more easily than those that don't. Some can even fight off these enemies with their powerful wings.

Despite all these advantages, only three groups of animals have wings: all birds, all bats, and almost all types of insects.

Only animals with wings can truly fly. The flying squirrel doesn't have wings. It uses flaps of skin to glide short distances from tree to tree.

The flying fish doesn't have wings either. It has special fins that let it leap out of the water and glide. But, like the flying squirrel, it can't travel very far.

Birds have wings made of several bones and different kinds of feathers. To keep the wings in good shape, birds *molt*—they regularly lose the old, worn feathers and grow new ones.

The bones in a bird's wing are similar to the bones in a human arm and hand. In humans these bones are solid. In birds that fly these bones are light and hollow. A bird's hand has just three fingers, and its palm and wrist are joined together. You cannot see its hand because a bird's feathers cover and extend far beyond it.

Like an airplane, a bird has curved wings to help it stay in the air. Air flows faster over the curve and pulls the wings upward. Air flows slower under the curve and pushes it up. The bird flaps its wings to make more air flow so that it can rise higher. It uses its large, strong chest and shoulder muscles to move its wings in flight. The shape of its wings can tell you what kind of flying it does and also what kind of life it leads.

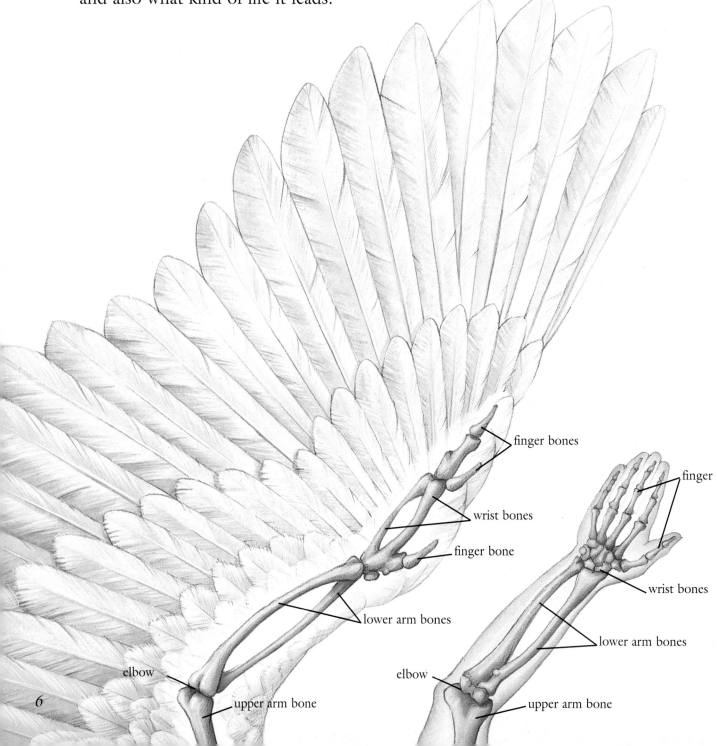

finger bones

finger

wrist bones

finger bone

wrist bones

lower arm bones

lower arm bones

elbow

elbow

6

upper arm bone

upper arm bone

Seabirds such as the albatross and the frigate bird have very long, narrow wings to help them soar over the oceans on rising air currents. From this height they search the water below for fish and other food. The wandering albatross has the longest *wingspan* of any bird—from ten to twelve feet long.

Eagles, hawks, and vultures have broader, somewhat shorter wings that let them soar on different air currents high over land to scan for mice and other *prey* on the ground.

wandering albatross

black vulture

barn owl

bald eagle

barn swallow

hummingbird

Owls' wings are more rounded than those of eagles, hawks, and vultures. This gives the owl a faster takeoff and lets it move more easily among trees. An owl's feathers are also softer, with brushy edges, so that the owl's flight is silent—all the better to surprise prey.

great horned owl

barn swallows

hummingbird

Emperor penguins

Swifts and swallows have slim, crescent-shaped wings. This shape allows them to twist, turn, and zip through the air as they hunt flying insects.

The hummingbird can move its brightly colored wings in almost any direction to fly forward, backward, sideways, or up and down. It can also *hover* in one spot to sip nectar from flowers. When it hovers, a hummingbird beats its wings up to seventy-five times a second, making the hum that gives this bird its name.

A penguin's wings are its flippers. They are covered with many short feathers. The bird uses these flippers to fly through water instead of air.

9

ostrich

Even though all birds have wings, not all birds can fly.

The ostrich's wings look like gigantic fans—and act like them, too. Too big and heavy to fly, the ostrich runs instead, using its wings for balance. To cool off, the bird faces the wind and flaps its wings to raise a breeze.

On the Galápagos Islands, the Galápagos cormorant once had no enemies. It didn't need to escape. So, over thousands of years, its wings got smaller and smaller until it became a flightless bird.

Most chickens can't fly either—because people haven't wanted them to. Many years ago, people bred birds that would stay put in their farmyards, gardens, and coops to lay eggs and provide meat. These birds are the ancestors of our chickens today.

Galápagos cormorant

spur-winged goose

hoatzin

Birds' wings aren't just for flying.

Many birds use their wings as weapons. A pigeon will snap out a stiff wing to hit an enemy or a rival pigeon. The spur-winged goose has wings that are even more threatening. There is a spike on top of each one.

In South America, young hoatzins have two hooked claws on their wings. The claws look like weapons but aren't. They allow the chicks to grip twigs as they explore the treetops where they nest.

In Africa, the black heron stands still in ponds or rivers and raises its wings like a big umbrella. This strange behavior probably cuts down on sun glare so that the heron can more easily see and catch fish and other prey.

black heron

blue bird of paradise

Many birds raise, flap, flutter, and show off their wings to court mates. Often their wings have amazing colors or markings. The male blue bird of paradise has a black back and sky blue wings. To attract a mate, he hangs upside down and spreads his gorgeous plumes. The sun bittern is a rather plain-looking bird that sits on forest floors and low branches. But when it opens its wings, it looks like a dazzling sunset.

Some birds protect their eggs or young with their wings. The killdeer fools *predators* by pretending it has a broken wing. It holds out a crooked wing and limps on the ground to lure enemies away from its nest. Then it flies off to make its own escape.

sun bittern

When it comes to wings, many people think of birds first, but birds weren't the first animals to fly. Insects were.

Most types of insects have two pairs of wings, but some have a single pair and others have no wings at all. Insect wings are made of thin skin called *membrane*. In many flies, grasshoppers, mantises, and other insects, the wings are transparent and you can see veins running through them. Scientists can identify different types of insects, such as dragonflies, lacewings, and many kinds of flies, by the patterns of veins in their wings.

Other insect wings are covered with tiny *scales*. Butterfly and moth wings get their color and beauty from thousands of these scales.

The earliest flying insects had two separate pairs of wings, the way a dragonfly does today. Ancestors of dragonflies lived millions of years ago. Some of them had wingspans that were almost three feet long.

Like a biplane, a dragonfly can skim, glide, and hover over land or especially water, where it catches other bugs for food. But it can't fold its wings when it rests. When it flies, each pair of a dragonfly's wings works separately. One pair flaps downward while the other pair beats upward, in an X shape. Large and strong, dragonflies are among the fastest insect fliers. Some can zoom along at sixty miles per hour. Although giant dragonflies no longer exist, dragonflies today still have long wings. Some types have wingspans of over seven inches.

But there are butterflies and moths with even longer wings. The white witch moth found in Central and South America has a twelve-inch wingspan—the longest of any insect. Like dragonflies, moths and butterflies have two sets of wings. But their wings are not separate. In most moths, they are held together by spines and bristles and in butterflies, by a type of lobe. This gives them more flexibility. They can also fold their wings to keep their bodies warm and to make themselves smaller targets for enemies.

green darter

red skimmer

bottle fly

diving beetle

green bottle fly

housefly

hairy-legged fly

green tiger beetle

diving beetle

The most flexible fliers, the fighter pilots of the insect world, are flies. They have just one set of wings. Their rear wings have turned into little movable clubs that keep the flies steady when they fly. These clubs and the fly's muscles allow it to do acrobatics in the air. It can swoop, dart, and rise quickly with ease. A housefly can even take off backward and sideways. Since predators usually attack head-on, this backward takeoff is a great way to escape. Flies can beat their wings very fast, as well. The tiny midge, for example, can beat its wings one thousand times a second.

You might not think that beetles fly, but they do. Their front wings are a hard cover that protects their more delicate hind wings while the bugs crawl around to feed, mate, and rest. Water beetles and other aquatic bugs also have wings. Why do insects that live underwater need wings? If their pond or stream dries up or gets polluted, these insects can fly away to a new home.

ladybug

Among insects, only the adults can fly. Some insects have wings for just a short time then lose them. Some ant queens have wings only during courtship. After they mate, these ants bite or rub off their wings and spend the rest of their lives flightless.

Just as bird wings are used for other things besides flying, so are insect wings. Male crickets sing with their wings to tell other crickets where they are and to attract mates. The warmer the temperature, the faster a cricket chirps.

In very hot weather all the honeybees in a hive will beat their wings to air-condition their home. They also beat them to evaporate water from the nectar they gather from flowers to turn it into honey.

bush cricket

peanut head bug

peanut head bug

18

Wings can also be *camouflage*. They may look like leaves, flowers, or tree bark to hide insects from predators. Or they may startle predators with strange coloring or spots that resemble big eyes. The yellow-winged locust flashes its yellow rear wings in flight. Then the insect folds its wings, drops to the ground, and hides while the enemy is still searching for that bright yellow thing it saw just a moment before in the air. The monarch butterfly's orange-and-black wings warn birds that it tastes bad. Birds remember that pattern and leave these butterflies alone. The viceroy butterfly *mimics* the monarch: it looks a lot like the other butterfly to fool predators into thinking that it tastes bad, too.

A butterfly's wing color may also help the insect stay at the right temperature. Dark colors absorb sunlight, so butterflies in cooler places often have darker wings to keep them warm. Butterflies in warmer climates may have lighter wings to reflect sunlight and stay cool.

phyllophora
bush cricket

bush cricket

Jacoba silk moth

shield bug

leaf insect

19

We can hear many birds and insects when they flap, whirr, or beat their wings. But bats fly silently—and most of them fly at night. That may be why some people are afraid of them. The truth is most bats are helpful. As they zip through the air, insect-eating bats zap pests, such as mosquitoes and moths.

Mammals are furred animals that nurse their babies with milk, and a bat is the only mammal with wings. Like a bird's wings, a bat's wings are its forearms and hands. A bat's wing has four very long fingers and one short one covered with two layers of leathery membrane. This membrane is not only strong, but it heals easily if it gets injured. When bats fly, they stretch out their arms and move their fingers to change the shape of their wings and control their flight.

Bumblebee bats, the smallest of all bats and the smallest mammal in the world, have wings just five inches long from tip to tip. Some of the big bats called flying foxes have wingspans of six feet.

brown bat

horseshoe bat

vampire bat

Bats can dive, flutter, and hover, but they can't soar. They move their wings the way people move their arms when they're rowing a boat, but bats push and pull through the air, not through water. Insect-eating bats have narrower, shorter wings so they can change direction easily and avoid obstacles. The heavier fruit-eating bats fly more slowly, but they can also fly farther to find food.

dwarf epauletted bat

Insect-eating bats also use their wings to catch prey. They net the insects with their wings, pulling the prey into their mouths. Bats can identify different types of insects by detecting how fast they beat their wings. For smaller bats, this is very important because they can't catch bugs that are too big.

When bats nest, they hang upside down and often wrap their wings around themselves for protection. The wings make a good raincoat. They may also camouflage the bats, making them look like leaves or stones. Short-tailed bats, which nest in caves, burrows, hollow trees, and decaying logs, have special pouches to protect their folded wings from damage. The pouches are made of a thick membrane on the bat's sides. The bat rolls its wings beneath the membrane.

horseshoe bat

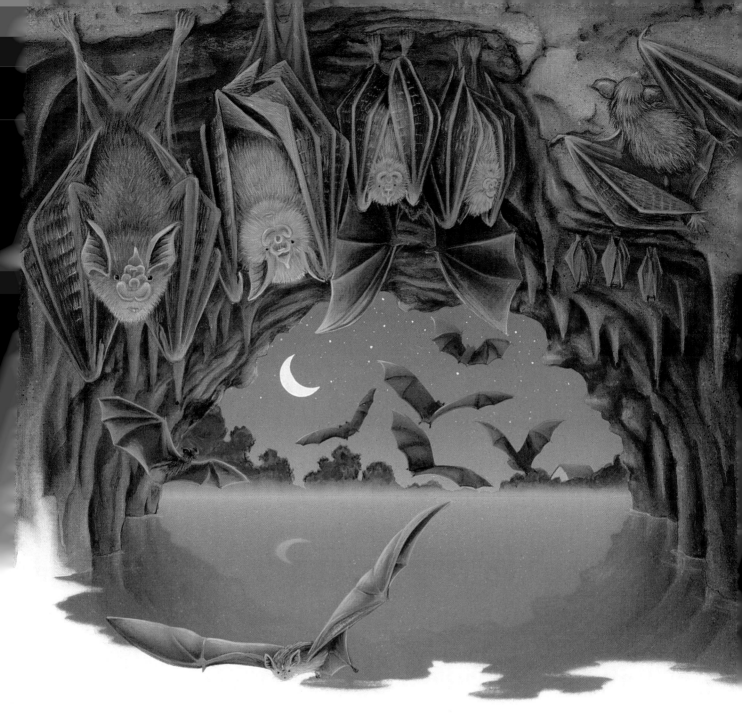

Like birds, some bats use their wings as weapons, striking at enemies. Male greater white-lined bats fight over *territory*. Their wings have *scent glands*. They wave them to release the smell and mark their turf.

Other males use their wings to attract females. Male hammer-headed bats gather in groups of about one hundred to sing and flap their wings quickly. The females hover among them to choose their mates.

Although all bats—unlike all birds—can fly, some spend a lot of time on the ground. The lesser short-tailed bat from New Zealand uses its folded wings to dig, walk, run, and climb. It rarely flies for more than a few miles.

But flying is what most animals do with their wings. Many birds, some bats, and a few insects fly very far indeed. They *migrate,* traveling spring and fall to places where they can find food and the right climate to live and breed. Flying uses much less energy to cover long distances than walking or running, and, of course, it takes much less time. So the most famous migrators are mainly animals with wings.

Birds travel the most miles. Among them, the arctic tern holds the record for the longest migration. It flies eleven thousand miles twice a year.

Mexican free-tailed bats don't travel nearly as far as arctic terns, but they travel in larger groups, from Mexico to Texas, New Mexico, and other states. Each spring groups of hundreds of thousands of females fly to Austin, Texas, to give birth. Each female has one baby. By midsummer there are over one million bats living under the Congress Street Bridge. In a single night these bats can eat ten to thirty million pounds of insects. The bats head back down south in the fall.

Some butterflies, such as the painted lady and the buckeye, migrate to find food or to escape cold or drought. But they don't always migrate every year. The monarch is the only butterfly known to make a regular round-trip. In the fall, monarchs fly south to Mexico or California to spend the winter. Some travel nearly two thousand miles—all the way from southern Canada to central Mexico. Each spring they start the return journey, laying eggs along the way. The old butterflies die, but their eggs hatch into caterpillars. The caterpillars turn into the butterflies that will continue the voyage north. The grandchildren of these butterflies will complete the migration circle in autumn.

Next time you see a butterfly, a bird, or a bat, think about these journeys, both long and short. Think about where you would go and what you would do if, like them, you could take to the air on a pair of wondrous wings.

Winged creatures are all around us. Pigeons, honeybees, houseflies, and swallows may be familiar to you. Mexican free-tailed bats, viceroys, arctic terns, and hoatzins may not be. You probably know that mosquitoes are pests. But do you also know that bats, dragonflies, warblers, and many other animals hunt these pests? Some of these animals are in danger because people fear them or don't understand how important they are. We cut down forests, pollute rivers and lakes, and destroy their habitats in other ways. We may even kill animals we don't understand. Not only do the animals lose, but so do we.

You can help by learning about these animals. Reading is one way to find out about them. Watching closely is another way. Go to a park, a lake, a river, a forest, or even your backyard. How many animals with wings can you see in a day? How long can you watch a single creature? What do you know about that animal? What do you see when you watch it? The more you look, the more you'll want to look. The more you know, the more you'll want to know. You'll discover what place each animal has in the world. That's a good thing for you and for winged creatures everywhere.

GLOSSARY

camouflage—The shape, colors, and patterns of an animal that let it blend into its surroundings. Camouflage disguises an animal so that predators cannot easily see it.

hover—To hang in place in the air. Animals hover by beating their wings rapidly.

mammal—An animal that nurses its young with milk and is covered with hair or fur. Mammals breathe through their lungs and are warm-blooded—they have a constant body temperature no matter what the air temperature is.

membrane—A thin layer of skin that can sometimes be seen through.

migrate—To make a seasonal journey to escape heat or cold and to find enough food. Bird, bat, and butterfly migrations usually take place each spring and fall.

mimic—To copy the appearance of another animal. To fool predators some animals mimic others that smell or taste bad.

molt—To lose and replace old, worn feathers. Birds generally molt once or twice a year to keep their wings in good shape.

predator—An animal that catches and eats other animals.

prey—An animal that is hunted by a predator for food.

scale—One of many small skinlike bits that cover butterfly and moth wings. Scales give the wings strength, color, and shine.

scent gland—The part of an animal's body that can make and give off an odor. The odor is used to attract mates, mark territory, or scare away enemies.

territory—The area that an animal calls home. Many animals will defend their territory against other animals, including their own kind.

wingspan—The length of outstretched wings from tip to tip.

ORGANIZATIONS

There are many good organizations that work to protect and educate about wildlife. Here are just a few of them. You can call or write to them for information or explore their websites. Many of these sites have links to other worthwhile organizations or other sites just for kids.

American Museum of Natural History
Central Park West at 79th St.
New York, NY 10024
212-769-5100
http://www.amnh.org

Bat Conservation International
P.O. Box 162603
Austin, TX 78716
512-327-9721
http://www.batcon.org

Defenders of Wildlife
1101 14th St. NW, #1400
Washington, DC 20005
202-682-9400
http://www.defenders.org

Greenpeace USA
1436 U Street NW
Washington, DC 20009
800-326-0959
http://www.greenpeaceusa.org

National Audubon Society
700 Broadway
New York, NY 10003
212-979-3000
http://www.audubon.org

The Nature Conservancy
4245 North Fairfax Dr.,
Suite 100
Arlington, VA 22203
703-841-5300
http://www.tnc.org

North American Butterfly
Association
4 Delaware Rd.
Morristown, NJ 07960
http://www.naba.org

Sierra Club
85 Second St., 2nd Floor
San Francisco, CA 94105
415-977-5500
http://www.sierraclub.org

Wildlife Conservation Society
2300 Southern Blvd.
Bronx, NY 10460
718-220-5111
http://www.wcs.org

World Wildlife Fund
1250 24th St. NW
Washington, DC 20037
800-225-5993
http://www.worldwildlife.org

The Xerces Society
4828 SE Hawthorne Blvd.
Portland, OR 97215
503-232-6639
http://www.xerces.org

Zoological Society of San Diego
P.O. Box 120551
San Diego, CA 92112
619-432-3153 (zoo)
760-738-5057 (park)
http://www.sandiegozoo.org

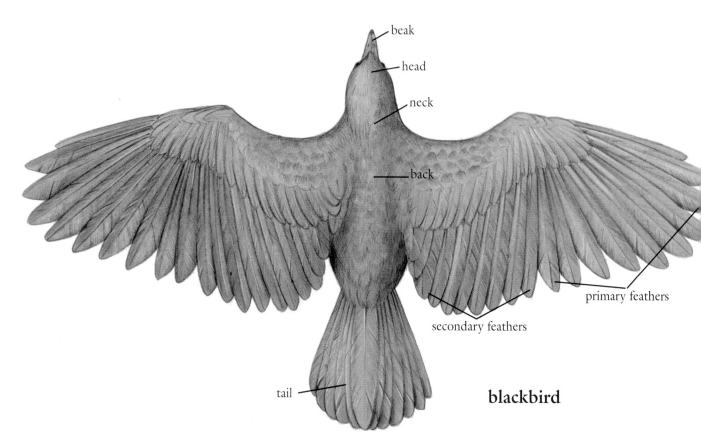

beak

head

neck

back

primary feathers

secondary feathers

tail

blackbird

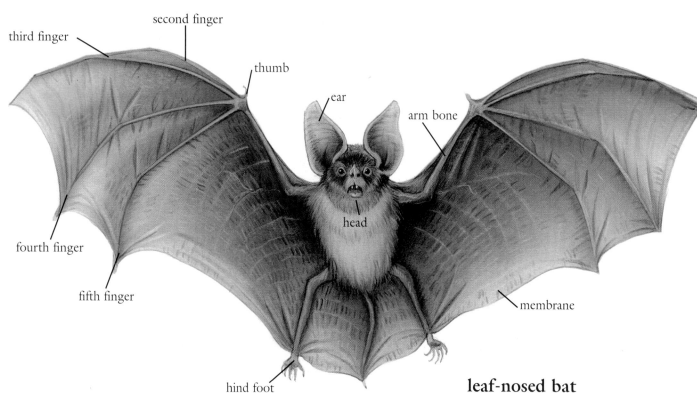

third finger

second finger

thumb

ear

arm bone

fourth finger

fifth finger

head

hind foot

membrane

leaf-nosed bat

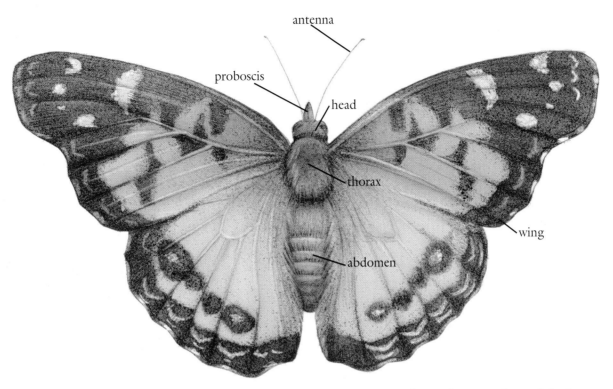

antenna

proboscis

head

thorax

wing

abdomen

American painted lady

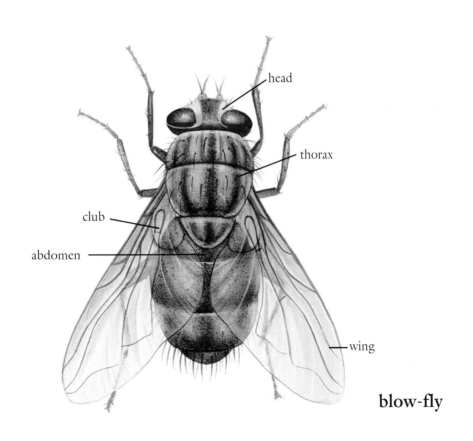

head

thorax

club

abdomen

wing

blow-fly

SOME GOOD BOOKS

Ackerman, Diane. *Bats: Shadows in the Night*, New York: Crown Publishers, 1997.

Arnold, Caroline. *Bat*. New York: Morrow Junior Books, 1996.

Fischer-Nagel, Heiderose & Andreas. *The Housefly*. Minneapolis: Carolrhoda Books, 1990.

Lasky, Kathryn. *Monarchs*. San Diego: Harcourt Brace, 1993.

Markle, Sandra. *Outside and Inside Bats*. New York: Atheneum, 1997.

Outside and Inside Birds. New York: Atheneum, 1995.

McLaughlin, Molly. *Dragonflies*. New York: Walker & Co., 1989.

Patent, Dorothy Hinshaw. *Feathers*. New York: Cobblehill Books, 1992.

Pringle, Laurence. *An Extraordinary Life: The Story of a Monarch Butterfly*. New York: Orchard Books, 1997.

Simon, Seymour. *Ride the Wind: Airborne Journeys of Animals and Plants*. San Diego: Browndeer Press, 1997.

INDEX